A novelization by B.B. Hiller
Based on the motion picture written by Jim Strain

SCHOLASTIC INC.
New York Toronto London Auckland Sydney

TRI-STAR PICTURES PRESENTS "BINGO" CINDY WILLIAMS DAVID RASCHE
MUSIC BY JOHN MORRIS
WRITTEN BY JIM STRAIN PRODUCED BY THOMAS BAER DIRECTED BY MATTHEW ROBBINS
A TRI-STAR RELEASE
© 1991 TRI-STAR PICTURES, INC. ALL RIGHTS RESERVED

ISBN 0-590-45276-2

12 11 10 9 8 7 6 5 4 3 2   1 2 3 4 5 6/9

Printed in the U.S.A.   40

First Scholastic printing, August 1991

For Andy Hiller

Prologue

Once upon a time there was a dog, and his name was Bingo. Bingo looked like an ordinary dog, but he wasn't ordinary at all. The trouble was that some people were just too busy to notice how special he was.

Bingo lived with a circus. He belonged to a man named Steve who performed in the circus with his three trained poodles and his pony named Penny. Steve pampered his poodles and his pony. He didn't pamper Bingo.

"Where is that good-for-nothing mutt, Bingo?" Steve asked his wife Ginger. "I sent him to fill the bucket of water over thirty minutes ago! What's he doing — digging a well?"

Bingo was having fun playing with the clowns. He loved to watch them practice their acts. Even more, he loved to watch them put on their

1

makeup, especially if it meant they'd give him a lick of the cold cream they used. Bingo thought cold cream was delicious. Bingo stood up on his haunches and whined.

"All right, all right," one of the clowns said, holding out the jar of cold cream. Bingo lapped at it eagerly. "Don't they feed you over there?"

Bingo answered by licking his chops happily.

"Step on it, guys," another clown said. "Rehearsal time. It's almost eleven o'clock."

Eleven o'clock! That meant that Bingo was late bringing back the bucket of water and Steve would be fuming!

Bingo licked the last of the cold cream off his face and dashed out of the clowns' tent. He picked up his bucket in his teeth and raced to the faucet. A few turns of the handle with his paws and fresh water spewed from the spigot. As soon as it was full, he picked up the bucket again and headed for home. He didn't have a second to waste — he'd have to take a shortcut across Swami Rhamjani's bed of nails. It was a good thing the Swami was taking a nap. Bingo trotted right across him. The little dog dodged through the elephant cage, under the lions' trailer, around the fat lady, and under the trampoline. That brought him right up behind Penny the pony. He put the bucket down and barked to get Steve's attention.

It got Steve's attention, but it also got Penny's attention. The pony was so startled that she kicked the bucket over. That was what Steve saw when he turned around. It didn't make him happy.

"Why you good-for-nothing, flea-ridden, worm-carrying cyst! Look what you've done! You're hopeless!" He pulled a brown sack from under his trailer and held it up in front of Bingo's face.

"Remember this?" he asked. "Want to go back into the river where I found you?"

Bingo hung his head in shame. He'd let Steve down. He didn't like to do that to anybody. He whimpered. Steve was about to start yelling at him again when Ginger interrupted.

"Steve," she said, holding one of their poodles. "Something's wrong with Lauren!"

She put the poodle down on the ground. Lauren hobbled in pain. Steve had to put off yelling at Bingo. Lauren's foot was much more important.

The vet found the problem right away. Lauren had stepped on a nail from the Swami's bed. The vet took his large tweezers and yanked it out.

"Look at the size of that thing!" Steve complained. "Why, when I get ahold of that guy Rhamjani, I'm going to take a hammer to his bed and then I'll — "

"Slow down, Steve," the vet said. "Your dog will be just fine. I'll put a bandage on her foot and she'll be ready to go in a couple of days."

"A couple of days!" Steve yelled. "I've got half of the people from the television network coming to the show tonight! They want a dog-and-pony-show for prime time. What am I going to do with just two dogs and a pony?"

"Use two dogs and a pony," the vet suggested.

"No way!" Steve growled. "You can't rip apart an act like this. The timing, the training. Without Lauren, we're dead!"

"Why not use Bingo?" Ginger suggested.

"Bingo?" he said.

There was a roll of drums. The lights in the circus tent dimmed. The audience was quiet, anticipating a great event. A small flame touched the edge of a large hoop and in an instant, the whole hoop burst into a fiery ring, illuminating the circus stage.

A single spotlight clicked on, focusing on a small empty platform. Steve stood next to it, dressed in his show outfit. He slapped his riding crop against his leg.

"Come on, come on," he hissed anxiously.

Bingo looked down at himself. He was wearing

all of Lauren's sparkles, including a rhinestone collar and tiara. He felt dumb enough at that, but it was nothing compared to how he felt about the tulle ballet skirt Ginger had fastened around his midsection.

Ginger gave him a little shove. Reluctantly, he entered the ring and climbed up onto the platform. There was applause.

"Jump!" Steve whispered, clipping at Bingo's hindquarters with the riding crop.

Bingo barely heard the words. At that moment, he wasn't even aware of his dumb costume. All his attention was focused on the fiery hoop in front of him. Flames licked upward, threatening, bright fiery yellow, red, and blue. Flames, he remembered, like the ones in the pet store when he was just a little puppy. Flames like the ones that had killed his mother. Flames like the ones that had changed his life forever. Flames.

Bingo couldn't move.

People in the audience started laughing.

"Jump, you stupid dog!" said Steve.

Bingo wasn't stupid — just scared. Flames had ruined his life once. He couldn't let it happen again.

Somebody in the audience threw popcorn at Steve and Bingo. Bingo didn't notice. Steve did.

All Bingo saw were flames. All Steve saw was his career going up in smoke.

"There it was! All those men from the TV network! We had a chance at prime time!" he yelled at Ginger later in their trailer. "I could see it! My own series! Spin-offs! Plush toys! All of it ruined because that stupid dog deliberately ruined my act!"

Ginger held Bingo tenderly. He cringed in her arms. "You're wrong, Steve," Ginger said. "Something about that fire scared him."

Bingo had always thought that Ginger was smarter than Steve.

"Well, I've got the cure!" Steve said. He pulled a shotgun out of his closet. "It's time I did him and the world a big favor!"

"Run, Bingo! Run for cover!" Ginger cried.

Obediently, Bingo leapt out of her arms. In a second he returned, bringing the covers from her bed!

"No, Bingo, not covers! Escape! Run for freedom! Do whatever makes you happiest!"

Bingo dropped the covers and ran back into the bedroom. He knew just the thing that made him happiest, and he brought it out to Ginger. It was a tennis ball!

"Not playful happy — fulfilling happy. Start a new life. Find a family."

Bingo knew what a family was. Ginger had one, and their picture was on her bedside table. There were her mom and dad, her brother Tim, and her sister Beth. He took the picture to Ginger, but she wasn't happy to see it at all. In fact, she seemed totally frustrated.

"No, you idiot! Not my family! Your *own* family." The look on Bingo's face made it clear he didn't understand. Ginger was at the end of her rope. "You're right," she said to Steve. "Let's kill him." She yanked the shotgun from his hand.

Then Bingo understood. It was time to go — *fast!*

It was time to start over — again.

1

"**W**ait up guys!" twelve-year-old Chuckie Devlin yelled. He was on his bicycle, trying to keep up with his older stepbrother and his stepbrother's friends. They were making it very hard for Chuckie. It was something his fourteen-year-old stepbrother often did, and the fact that their names were almost the same didn't help. His stepbrother's name was Chickie.

The older kids had just jumped a small stream on their bikes. Now they expected Chuckie to do the same. If Chuckie had been walking, he would have thought it was easy, but on a bike, it was something else. He stared at the expanse of water.

"What are you afraid of, dorkmeier?" Chickie taunted him.

"Nothing," Chuckie lied, but he didn't move.

"Let's go guys. He's choked," Chickie said. He and his friends rode off.

Chuckie took a deep breath. If Chickie could jump the stream, he was sure he could — or at least he was sure he had to try. He backed up his bike, aimed, and began pedaling as hard as he could. He rode up the rock Chickie and his friends had used to launch themselves. He gave an extra hard push on his pedals and flew into the air.

It seemed to Chuckie that he hung in midair forever, soaring over the wide span of the stream. But then his front wheel hit a rock in the middle of the stream and crashed, throwing Chuckie right toward the muddy water. Before he splashed into it, his head hit another rock. He was out like a light.

Bingo heard the crash. One look over the edge of the roadway and he knew he had to help. He dropped his knapsack and dashed down the hill. The boy was completely unconscious and was lying facedown in the water. There wasn't a second to spare. He got a good grip on Chuckie's pant leg and tugged, pulling him up the bank of the stream. As soon as he was out of the water, Bingo put his snout under Chuckie's chest and pushed hard until the boy rolled over on his back. He lay lifelessly with his mouth open. Bingo put an ear to Chuckie's chest. He could hear a faint heartbeat. Then he checked for breathing. Nothing! He had to think fast!

Chuckie was lying next to the rock he'd used for a jump ramp. Bingo climbed up onto it and jumped right onto Chuckie's chest. It was an airborne Heimlich maneuver and just what Chuckie needed. He coughed and gasped. He was alive! He threw up. Then he fainted.

When Chuckie opened his eyes, he was at a campsite. All of his own clothes were hung neatly on a line, next to a dog collar.

He put on his jeans and then looked at the dog collar. It had a tag on it.

" 'Bingo,' " he read out loud.

"Woof!" came an answer from the pup tent. Then Bingo appeared. He was a scruffy-looking mutt, but as far as Chuckie was concerned, he was the most beautiful dog in the world.

"Yours?" Chuckie asked, holding up the collar.

Bingo nodded and came over to Chuckie, allowing him to put the collar back on him.

"You saved my life, didn't you, fella?" Chuckie asked.

Bingo nodded again.

"All right, high five!" Chuckie said. Paw met hand triumphantly.

"You're amazing! Where did you come from? Whatever, you and I are going to be friends for life, right boy?"

Bingo knew what friends did together when one was a dog and the other was a boy. They played! Obligingly, Bingo offered Chuckie a stick to throw so he could fetch it.

Chuckie laughed warmly. "Not now, boy," he said. "First I've got to get something to eat. I'm starved."

Bingo dashed off and before Chuckie could get his T-shirt on, the little mutt was back — with a fish in his mouth!

"Whoa! You really are something!" Chuckie said, taking the fish from Bingo, although the idea of eating a raw fish had limited appeal. He didn't want to hurt Bingo's feelings. He took a few tentative nibbles and then saw the look in the dog's eyes.

"It's delicious, but why don't you finish it?" Chuckie suggested. Bingo seemed very grateful for it and began gnawing at it right away. Chuckie finished getting dressed. He talked as he tied his shoes.

"I have to take you home now, but there are just two problems to that — Mom and Dad. No pets allowed, see. Oh, and there's a third problem — Chickie. He's my older brother, sort of. What he is, is my stepdad's real son before he got married to my mom, who's not my real mom because I'm adopted."

Bingo whined. Chuckie could tell he was confused.

"Yes, we've got a complicated family," Chuckie said apologetically. He was going to go on and explain about steps and adoptions, but he was interrupted by a nearby growl. It was a big growl and it came from a big bear who had rambled into the little campsite.

"Sic 'em, Bingo!" Chuckie yelled, backing away from the approaching animal. But Bingo was nowhere to be seen. "Bingo?"

Bingo barked. He was safely up a tree! He barked again and pointed with his nose to the half-eaten fish.

Chuckie understood. He picked up the fish and tossed it to the bear. When the bear was distracted enough by the food, Chuckie shinnied up the tree and sat on a branch next to Bingo. The two of them hugged one another for comfort. They clung to one another for hours. Every time

Chuckie started to think it would be all right to come down, the bear growled and changed Chuckie's mind.

Night fell. Chuckie sang to comfort himself and his dog.

"There was a kid who had a dog, and Bingo was his name-o! B-I-N-G — "

"Woof!" Bingo supplied.

"B-I-N-G — "

"Woof!"

"B-I-N-G — "

"Woof!"

"And Bingo was his — "

"Woof! Woof!"

Chuckie was having so much fun, he almost forgot how scared he was of the bear who still growled nearby.

"No sweat, Bingo. Someone'll come looking for us. It won't be long," he assured the dog. Then he decided to try something else.

"Heeeeeelllllllppppp!" he yelled.

There was no answer.

2

Chickie and his mom and dad, Natalie and Hal Devlin, sat at the dining room table. Each of them was very aware of the empty chair. And each, in their own way, was worried.

Dad was worried about the fact that, as a field goal kicker for the Denver Broncos, he was doing a lousy job. He also wondered where Chuckie was.

Mom was worried that some of the bets she'd made at the racetrack had cost her a lot of money, and Dad's failure as a football player wasn't going to make it easy to make up the lost cash. She, too, was uncomfortable about the fact that Chuckie wasn't home yet.

Chickie was worried about Chuckie. He was worried that he'd get blamed if something happened to the little brat.

Mom picked up the platter of chicken and offered it to Chickie.

"More chuckie," she said, stumbling over the words. "I mean chicken, Chuck. No, I mean chicken, Chick. Chicken, Chickie!" she said finally.

Chickie looked to his father for help.

"Finish your chuckin, Chickie. Chicken, Chuck. Chicken, Chickie!" he said. It was never easy when they had chicken for dinner. "Besides," Dad added. "I wanted pizza!"

"Chuck E. Cheese?" Chickie joked.

Dad didn't think it was funny. He threw his napkin on the table. "I don't need your attitude! I've had a tough day!"

"Look, buster, don't start in with him. He didn't miss those field goals!" Mom said.

Dad looked sadly at his bare foot. "You don't understand. Nobody understands."

"Leave your foot on the floor and the game at the stadium," Mom said. "Right now, I'm worried about our son."

"Even if he is adopted," Chickie added.

"He's one of the family," Mom and Dad said together.

"Well he's probably just messing around in the woods," Chickie told his parents. He didn't tell them about leaving Chuckie to jump the stream all by himself. "Anyway, why do I always get chewed out when Chuckie's the one in trouble?"

"See! Even Chickie thinks Chuckie's in trouble!" Mom said to Dad.

"Will everybody cork it!" Dad said, nearly shouting. "If we don't hear anything by morning, I'll call the police."

"Morning?!"

"Morning!" Dad said with finality. "Now, pass the chucken!"

3

Natalie Devlin looked out of her bedroom window, waiting for the sun to come up. She and Dad had had a sleepless night, waiting for Chuckie. Dad still insisted he wouldn't call the police until dawn.

She glanced at the clock. "I don't care what the paper said. That's daylight out there. I'm calling the police!"

She reached for the phone, but then she saw a long shadow appear on the street. It was a boy on his bicycle. It was Chuckie!

"I told you he'd be back," Dad said. "And I'm going to rip his arms off!"

"Hal, no!" Mom said. "Remember, no more negative attention."

"How about just *one* arm?" Dad suggested.

* * *

Chuckie looked around. It looked clear. He whistled for Bingo. The dog dashed toward him from between some parked cars. Then he made a sharp turn to the right, veering off to the neighbor's yard, much more interested in the neighbor's cocker spaniel than in Chuckie's kitchen door.

"Hey, dude, this ain't the time to be thinking about girls!" Chuckie hissed at him. Reluctantly, Bingo abandoned the pretty golden-haired spaniel and joined Chuckie in the house.

At first, it seemed like everything was quiet, but then there was the sound of feet on the backstairs. Quickly, Chuckie shoved Bingo into a cabinet.

"Morning son. Sleep well?" Dad greeted Chuckie.

A little while later, Chuckie found himself sitting at the breakfast table, looking at the backs of everybody else's reading material. Dad was looking at the sports section, trying to ignore the headline that read DEVLIN SLUMP CONTINUES. Mom was, as usual, reading the racing form. Chickie was reading a comic book.

"Doesn't anybody want to know where I was?" Chuckie asked. "Do I need to appear on a milk carton first?"

"Finish your breakfast, Chuckie," Dad said. "I don't want you late for school."

"But shower first," Mom told him. "You smell like a wet dog."

"That's because of the toxic waste dump I fell into," Chuckie said, glaring at Chickie. But Chickie didn't notice. Nobody did. They didn't notice when Bingo snatched a sausage from the floor. They didn't notice when Chuckie slipped a slice of toast into the cabinet. Chuckie was a little relieved that nobody seemed to notice anything because that meant he was getting away with hiding Bingo. But he was also hurt, because it seemed like nobody cared.

"For all you care, I could have been kidnapped last night," he said.

"Pass the jam, Natalie," Dad said.

"What if I'd fallen into the hands of international terrorists?"

"More egg whites, Hal?"

Chuckie stood up and snuck Bingo out of the cabinet, aiming for the stairs.

"Hey, just a minute there!" Dad said.

Had he been found out already? Chuckie froze.

"I'm supposed to shower, aren't I?" he asked nervously.

"Aren't we forgetting something?" Dad asked. He reached out and tousled Chuckie's hair. "Chuckie, Chuckie, bring me luckie!" he recited.

Chuckie heaved a sigh of relief and made tracks up the backstairs.

4

The last thing Chuckie saw before he climbed into the car next to his mother was Bingo at his bedroom window, waving good-bye. When Chuckie was sure his mother couldn't see, he waved back.

"Here's your latchkey," Mom said to Chuckie when they pulled up in front of the school. "Don't forget to turn on the oven when you get home after school. It'll take those potatoes an hour to bake and I'll be at the racetrack until late. Wish me luck, huh?"

"Sure, Mom, good luck. But you know, some people think animals are good luck — "

"Forget it. No pets," she said, and then drove away.

At least he tried.

* * *

When he was satisfied that he was alone in the house, Bingo started to explore.

First stop was Mom and Dad's room. The water bed was lots of fun to walk on, but not very good for jumping. He made a note to try napping on it later. Then he spotted Mom's cosmetics on the dressing table. He trotted over to it and sniffed curiously. There were a lot of things there that reminded him of the clowns at the circus. Best of all, there was cold cream —

And that was just the beginning of a wonderful day.

"Bingo, I'm ho-ome!" Chuckie called before he opened the door. He didn't have to call it twice. The instant he opened the door, Bingo dashed between his legs to the nearest tree where he relieved himself. "Oh, yeah," Chuckie said. "I guess we've got to figure out a way for you to get out in the daytime, huh? That can wait until to-morrow, though. Because today, we're going to jam!"

And they did. Bingo was everything Chuckie ever could have hoped for — and more — in a dog. That afternoon, they did everything to-gether. First, they went to the arcade. Chuckie won at Mega Monster, but Bingo beat him hands down at Sky Dogs. Then it was time for some skateboarding. All it took was a few short lessons, and Bingo was as good as Chuckie. They soared around the neighborhood and Chuckie was sure Bingo was having as much fun as he was. At the local newsstand, Chuckie flipped through *X-Men* comics. Bingo chose *Lady and the Tramp*.

Then it was time for some homework. Chuckie found a nice shady tree and the two of them sat underneath it. Chuckie took a piece of paper and a pencil and opened his math book.

"If a wheat field yields forty-six bushels per acre and the farmer is able to harvest one-hundred thirty-eight bushels before a rainstorm, how many acres of wheat has he cut?" Chuckie read. He chewed on his pencil while he thought about how to solve the problem.

Bingo chewed thoughtfully on a stick for a second. Then he pawed the ground three times.

"Hey, yeah, right! Three acres! Thanks, boy!" Chuckie said, and he really meant it. They were friends for life and Chuckie thought nothing could ever spoil that.

5

"**H**ey, everybody! I'm ho-ome!" Chuckie called brightly, entering the front door. Bingo was safely shooed up the backstairs. They'd had such a wonderful time together that it seemed to Chuckie that nothing could ever go bad. He was wrong.

"Something got into my cold cream!" his mother complained, holding up her empty jar.

"Something chewed up my citizenship award!" Chickie growled, holding up several pieces of his plaque.

"And something soiled our driveway!" Dad howled, lifting his bare foot so Chuckie could imagine what had happened. It wasn't a pleasant thought.

Chuckie could feel himself breaking out in a sweat. His stomach felt totally hollow and his knees were weak. Had he been found out?

"What are you saying? That I'm hiding a — a dog?"

"Bingo!" his father said.

Chuckie gulped. Then he realized that it was just by chance his father had said Bingo. There was no way —

"Sooner or later, we're going to find him and when we do . . ." Chickie threatened.

"That's enough, Chickie. I'll do the threatening around here!" Dad turned to Chuckie. "You! Go to your room and pack your bags."

"Pack!" Chuckie said. "Don't you think you're overreacting a little?"

"Now!" Dad howled.

Chuckie turned for the stairs. He even took two steps before the truth dawned on him. He stopped and turned around.

"We've been traded again, haven't we?"

One of the problems with having a father who played professional football — and who was slumping — was that his teams traded him often, which meant moving the whole family across the country on a minute's notice.

"We leave first thing in the morning for Wisconsin," Mom said.

"Green Bay! I knew it!" Chuckie said dismally.

26

"Just when we were getting settled. Talk about quick on the trigger!"

"That's enough!" his mother scolded. "Your father needs support, not criticism. Now, upstairs!"

Chuckie fled. He knew the drill. He was supposed to pack enough clothes for a few days.

"The movers will take care of the rest," his mother said, handing him a pile of jeans.

"Can they take care of my insecurity? My lack of a stable environment? My sense of loss? My . . . my . . ." He searched for a word.

"Dog?" his mother supplied. It was, of course, just what he'd had in mind. "Chuckie, I know you don't make friends easily, but pets aren't the answer."

"You adopted me. Why not a pet?"

"Because pets smell. And claw furniture, and carry disease, and mess in the driveway. Maybe when you're older, we can get a fish." She handed him some socks to put in the footlocker.

"A fish! You can't hug a fish. You can't play ball with a fish. You can't fish with a fish. . . ."

"No," his mother said, closing the argument for the thousandth time.

"What's this?" Mom asked, her hand emerging from his sweatshirt drawer holding a handmade leather belt.

"It was supposed to be for Father's Day, but I screwed up on the footballs, which is why I gave Dad the after-shave."

"Why? This is beautiful!"

"My crafts teacher thought it was crummy."

"Your crafts teacher is not your father. And you know what? I think your Dad could really use some special cheering up right now. Why don't you go give it to him?"

That was one of those "suggestions" from Mom that was really an order. Chuckie took the belt and went into his parents' room where his father was packing his own clothes.

"Dad?" His father looked up. "I just wanted to say — Look, I like being traded, okay? New kids, new hangouts, new — weather. Anyway, I want you to have this. It was supposed to be for Father's Day, but . . ."

He handed the belt to his father. Dad smiled a little. "You made this?" he asked politely. Chuckie nodded. Dad examined it, obviously searching for something nice to say about it. "What are these round things here — acorns?"

"Footballs," Chuckie said.

"Close enough," Dad said quickly. "Nice work, son. I like it." He slid the belt through the loopholes on his pants and showed Chuckie that it fit almost perfectly.

It was a tender moment and Chuckie wasn't going to let it go to waste. "Things will get better, Dad. You'll see. All sorts of stuff can change your luck. Sometimes, when you need it the most, something special can come out of nowhere and make all the difference. Something warm, something frisky, something so full of love that — "

"Thanks for the belt, son, but we're not getting a dog."

So much for that bright idea.

6

Chuckie had everything set up just perfectly for Bingo. He'd drilled some holes in the side of his trunk and left enough room for Bingo to travel in style. What Chuckie hadn't allowed for was some companionship for Bingo, and Bingo needed that a lot right then. Images of the little cocker spaniel next door flashed through Bingo's mind. Who could resist a pretty face like that, deep brown eyes, cinnamon-colored whiskers, soft, silky ears, a look that could melt a pit bull? In the dark of night, Bingo emerged from the trunk at the foot of Chuckie's bed and made his way downstairs, where he borrowed a bottle of champagne from the Devlins' refrigerator, and out the door, where he found a nosegay of flowers in the Devlins' garden. Just the things he needed to woo a cute spaniel.

"Bingo! Bingo!" Chuckie called quietly. He was desperate to find the dog, but not so desperate he was going to give the secret away. It didn't matter, though. There was no sign of the dog — no secret to be given away.

He looked everywhere in the house, in the basement, in all the cupboards — even in the garbage can. No Bingo.

Mom shooed Chuckie into the station wagon, giving him the rear seat, facing backward. Chuckie was so heartbroken that he'd lost Bingo, sure that he'd lost him for good, that he barely noticed his father's feeble efforts to cheer him up.

"Buck up, son. Wisconsin's got great cheese!" he said, slamming the rear of the car closed.

No Bingo.

His father climbed into the driver's seat and turned on the engine.

No Bingo.

Bingo opened his eyes slowly, and lifted his chin off the back of the neck of the cocker spaniel. He sighed contentedly and rested his chin back down again.

There was a faint sound, a sound that meant trouble, but for a second, Bingo couldn't place it.

Then he knew. It was the sound of a car starting. It was the sound of Chuckie leaving!

In an instant, Bingo was up and running!

The car pulled out of the Devlins' driveway and turned onto the road. They were off.

Chuckie took one final look at the house and then he saw the dog dashing out of their neighbor's yard.

"Bingooooooo!" he cried. "Stop, Dad, stop!"

Dad looked in the rearview mirror. "I should have known! It's a dog!" he said and then stepped on the gas. "He'll never catch us now!"

"Speed up, Dad!" Chickie urged his father. Dad obliged.

Chuckie squinted, trying to see through his tears.

No Bingo.

7

Even when Bingo could no longer see the Devlins' station wagon, he could use his nose to tell him where it had gone. He sniffed and ran, sniffed and ran, sniffed and ran. Sometimes it was hard to tell whether he was sniffing or running faster. The only thing he knew for sure was that, with the possible exception of the cocker spaniel, Chuckie was the best thing that had ever happened to him, and he wasn't going to lose him now!

He cut through three yards, leaping over hammocks, scooting under fences. He blasted through shrubs, and flew down kiddie slides — anything to reach the main highway before the Devlins did.

He was fast, very fast, and he didn't have to stop for lights the way a station wagon did.

Maybe, just maybe, he could do it.

Then Bingo arrived at a large intersection. Six major roads met all at once. It was a sure thing that the Devlins would have to go through here, but had they already been? Bingo used his best weapon, his nose. With total disregard for his own safety, or for the gigantic traffic jam he caused by sniffing every inch of the intersection, Bingo proceeded. He just had to find the Devlins. He especially had to find Chuckie.

Horns blared and tempers flared. Bingo didn't notice and if he had, he wouldn't have cared. In fact, the only thing he did notice was when the long arm of the law reached out and snatched him by the collar.

The policeman looked Bingo square in the face. Then *he* sniffed suspiciously.

"What is that smell?" the policeman asked. "Have you been drinking?"

The champagne!

The next thing Bingo knew, the policeman had him walking along a narrow white line. Then he had to touch his snout with his paws, first his left, then his right, then left, then right. Finally, the policeman had him puffing into a breath-a-lyzer.

The policeman scanned the results of the tests.

"Well, you ain't drunk," he said. Bingo sighed

with relief. "So you must be dumb or crazy."

Both, Bingo thought.

"Listen pooch — chase cars again at this intersection and you wind up with three legs. You want to be a fuzzy brown spot next to the yellow line?"

Bingo shook his head vigorously.

"Well, you seem like a nice enough dog, so I'm going to let you off with a warning."

The policeman remounted his motorcycle and kick-started it. Much to Bingo's relief, he was gone.

Then there was a breeze out of the northeast. It wasn't much of a breeze, but it carried an unmistakable, familiar, and wonderful odor. Bingo was off like a shot, with only one thing on his mind — Chuckie.

Duke's Down Home Hot Dogs didn't seem like such a bad place for the Devlins to stop — until they were served.

"You've got to be kidding! This is stadium food!" Mom said.

"It's Americana," Dad assured her. "These little places are getting scarce. You boys are going to try some roadside-trucker cuisine before it disappears forever."

One sniff of his hot dog and Chuckie decided it

would be fine if it disappeared forever. He excused himself from the counter. He wanted to be outside where he might leave a scent that Bingo could pick up and follow.

There was a barn behind the restaurant. It was dilapidated and there was a lot of noise coming from it. Chuckie pulled the door open and went in. His eyes adjusted to the light slowly. It took a few minutes for him to realize that the whole place was stacked with crates and every one of the crates had a dog in it.

Duke, the owner of Duke's Down Home Hot Dogs, appeared from a small room at the end of the barn. He was wearing a cowboy outfit with expensive leather boots. He wore an apron over it and carried a large knife.

"Guaranteed fresh, pardner, or Duke'll give you your money back!"

The possible implications sunk in fast. Chuckie fainted.

When he awoke, he was back in the back of the station wagon. His father was trying to look at the bright side of their lunch. "So it wasn't blessed by Ronald McDonald. So what? Nothing a little mustard can't fix."

8

The going was rough for Bingo. He had no food, no water, plus he had a little bit of a hangover from the champagne. Nevertheless, he persevered. He put one paw in front of the other three and kept on going, driven by his devotion to his new friend for life, Chuckie.

The long gray road in front of him seemed to become wavy in the intense overhead sun. Vultures circled above him menacingly. Step by step, he proceeded.

A figure shimmered in the heat waves coming from the ground. Closer and closer it came, carrying a canteen. It looked like Chuckie. The figure opened the canteen. Out poured . . . sand.

The sand turned into a brown sack. Chuckie became Steve.

"You want water?" he taunted, brandishing the

sack in front of Bingo's face. "I know a river . . ."

"Steve, don't do it!" It was Ginger's voice. "Let me, instead!"

Then Bingo blacked out, completely lost in his hallucination. The first thing he was aware of when he awoke was water, real water, not sand. It was coming from a squirt gun and nothing had ever tasted so wonderful in his life. The next thing he noticed was a fancy pair of cowboy boots on the feet of the man who was giving him water.

"Found another stray, Duke?" a woman's voice asked. "This must be your lucky day."

"Get him some chow, darlin'," Duke said. "Come along little doggie." He shoved Bingo into a crate and snapped a lock on the door. Bingo was in Duke's doggie prison!

Within a matter of minutes, the prison grapevine was hard at work and Bingo realized what a desperate situation he was in. This man Duke was a butcher!

What Duke didn't count on, though, was that Bingo was brave, smart, and determined. Nothing was going to keep him from getting to Chuckie.

Bingo pushed aside his water bowl and found what the bull terrier in the cage next to his had promised — the beginning of a tunnel to freedom. If the longest journey begins with a single step, the longest tunnel begins with a single pawful of dirt. Bingo began his job with a single pawful.

A door slammed. The bull terrier barked a warning woof. Bingo slid his water bowl back over the hole and lay down on the pile of dirt, trying to look very casual. Duke walked into the cage area, carrying his cleaver, his eyes scanning the dogs in his prison. He smiled, walking toward Bingo! Then he shifted to the right a little. His target was Bingo's new friend, the bull terrier. Bingo was about to bark in protest when there was a shriek from the kitchen. Duke ran to see what was up. The waitress had spotted a cockroach.

There wasn't a second to waste. Bingo finished off his tunnel and scooted out to freedom. First, he looked longingly at the door, but he couldn't go yet. He couldn't abandon his new friends to their certain fate.

While Duke and the waitress argued about the roach (she thought roaches were disgusting, but she didn't mind the rats in the kitchen; after all, they were mammals), Bingo unfastened all the latches on the cages and freed all the dogs.

Then there was just one other thing to do. They waited for the return of Duke and his waitress. The pack of dogs greeted the pair with snarls and snaps. The two humans backed away from the dogs in terror — right into their own cages!

Clip, snap! They were locked in. What came next took some ingenuity and some strength. The dogs, working together in perfect unity, managed to get the caged humans onto the back of Duke's truck. All seemed lost when they realized the keys to the truck were in Duke's pocket and they weren't willing to risk his escape to get them out. Bingo had the answer, though. He got six of the dogs to push the truck from behind while he sat at the steering wheel.

As soon as they had the truck in motion, Bingo popped the clutch. The engine backfired and then turned over. It was going! Bingo aimed it straight for the sign, and then at the ramshackle cabin that had been Duke's restaurant. Bingo hopped out of the truck's cab at the last moment and joined his friends to watch Duke's own truck destroy his restaurant before it rambled on down the hillside and toward the cliff.

High paws all around. They were free at last — for good!

9

The Devlins spent another day on the road. They'd traveled hundreds of miles and every one of them took Chuckie further away from Bingo.

Chuckie was trying his best to leave a trail for the dog. He knew Bingo was smart and he knew if he could leave signs of himself, something to see, something to sniff, maybe, just maybe, Bingo would find him. At every possible opportunity, Chuckie got out of the car and left a calling card for Bingo. He'd had to go to the bathroom so often, his parents were beginning to think he was sick — insofar as they noticed him at all.

At night, in the motels, it was a different thing.

"Yessssssss! Again!" Dad called out excitedly.

He and Chickie were practicing field goals in the motel room — with the help of a practice net.

Chuckie returned to the room after a visit to the local bushes.

"Where have you been?" Mom asked. "It's your turn to snap."

"He's been out leaving a trail for that stupid dog of his," Chickie said.

"Could we get on with practice here?" Dad asked.

"Chuckie, I want you to forget about that dog. Put him totally out of your mind."

"He doesn't have a mind," Chickie interrupted.

"You should talk!" Chuckie retorted. "That dog is smarter than you. In fact, he's smarter than this whole family and *nothing's* going to keep us apart!"

"Hey, I'm trying to concentrate!" Dad complained, trying to line up the ball and the target with his eyes.

"You figure it out, son," Mom said. "We've averaged sixty miles an hour, times eight hours, times two days. How far away do you think he is?"

It was enough to overwhelm Chuckie. It was also enough to distract Dad.

"Hike!" Chickie said. Chuckie tossed the football to him.

Dad took six steps and whacked the football

with his bare foot. It soared — right towards the window!

Crash!

"Don't look at me," Chickie said. "The snap was high."

It was *always* Chuckie's fault.

10

Bingo spotted a trailer park just off the north-bound highway. He thought maybe he could find something to eat there. He began pawing through trash cans.

A flashlight beam flicked on and searched for him. Bingo couldn't hide from it and besides, he thought maybe somebody would take pity on him.

"It's only a dog, Eli," a man said. He sounded relieved.

"Getting a little nervous, aren't you, Lennie?" a harsh voice answered.

"Can you blame me?" Lennie asked, snapping off his flashlight.

"Okay, okay. So club the mutt and let's get some sleep."

"Club him!? He's not a harp seal. What's your problem, Eli? Didn't you have a dog when you were a kid?"

"What's next? Save the Whales?" Eli said sarcastically.

Bingo didn't want them to support Save the Whales — just Save Bingo. Instead of doing either, they argued some more.

"You know," Lennie said. "It wouldn't hurt you to sign a petition now and then."

"What for? We're felons! We can't vote!"

"That doesn't mean we can't contribute in other ways," Lennie said. Then he finally turned to Bingo. "I bet you're hungry, huh, fella?"

"*Woof!*"

"Smart, too!"

"What's smart about waking up the whole county?" Lennie asked.

"Oh, don't mind Eli," Lennie told Bingo. "His bark is worse than his bite."

Bingo wasn't of a mind to bother at all about Eli — as long as Lennie actually fed him. The hungry dog followed Lennie willingly through a maze of trailers and up into one the two men were apparently calling home. It looked to Bingo more like a junkyard with an incredible collection of empty beer and soda cans, pizza boxes, cigar butts, and potato chip bags. A second look made Bingo realize that the place was also cluttered with guns, bullets, explosives, and — Bingo blinked, he could barely believe his eyes — money sacks!

Bingo's mind raced — to the refrigerator. Lennie opened it. There wasn't much there for a dog, unless Bingo wanted to consider some moldy applesauce. Then Lennie spotted a box of Velveeta.

"Hey, I was going to use that for nachos!" Eli growled.

"Nachos! You need chips for nachos!" Lennie said.

Eli leaned back in his chair and reached for the door of the closet behind him. He turned the handle and the door swung open, revealing four people bound and gagged — a father, a mother, and two little girls.

"You got any chips?" Eli asked the woman.

She looked terrified and shook her head no.

"That's okay, folks," Lennie said, apparently trying to reassure them. "We'll be gone after breakfast."

Eli slammed the door on the frightened foursome.

"Forget the nachos," Lennie said. "Let's turn in. Big day tomorrow."

Eli and Lennie each swept the beer cans off a bed. Lennie tossed a shirt on the floor for Bingo. "You curl up on this, fellah," he said. Bingo barely heard him. His eyes were still glued to the closet door and the closet's astonishing contents.

Eli pulled a gun and cocked it. Bingo heard that.

"Get away from that door, mutt. Now go to sleep or I'll put you to sleep."

Bingo walked over to the shirt, circled twice, lay down, and closed his eyes, but he didn't go to sleep.

Within minutes, the whole trailer was filled with the resounding snores of the two exhausted robbers. There wasn't a sound from the closet. Bingo stood up cautiously and tiptoed out of the trailer.

Bingo looked up into the air. He knew just what he needed and he spotted it: a telephone pole. He followed the wires that came into the trailer park and quickly realized that they led to the rest room complex.

Bingo didn't hesitate. He ran right in. But one look at the surprised woman and he realized he'd made a terrible mistake. Embarrassed, he backtracked until he found the men's room.

There was the pay phone. He pushed a chair over to it, climbed up, and nudged the receiver with his nose until it tumbled off the hook.

Now for the hard part, he told himself, carefully pressing 911.

11

The console at the emergency control center lit up. A second later, the calling number flashed on the screen, followed by a locater map blinking the source of the incoming call. The operator put down her Twinkie and her *Soap Opera Digest* and pressed a switch.

"Nine-one-one! What's your problem?" she asked smartly.

She couldn't hear anything that made any sense. There was heavy breathing and then there was some barking. In fact, there was a lot of barking.

"All I can hear is your dog. But we've locked in your number and location. Are you in trouble?"

The dog barked again. Then she heard the electronic bips of telephone keys being pressed.

... --- ... ... --- ...

It sounded very strange. She turned to her partner. "Dan, I think I've got a prankster calling from a pay phone on I-80. What do you make of it?"

Dan switched to her extension. "Hello? Hello?" he asked.

... --- ... ... --- ...

"Give me your pencil!" he said. "It's Morse code!"

"*Woof!*"

The loud snoring overwhelmed the sound of Bingo's gnawing as he chewed through the ropes binding the family in the closet. One by one, they tiptoed out of their own trailer to freedom. They didn't make a sound, until the last little girl tripped on a beer can.

Eli was awake in a shot. He sat bolt upright and pointed his gun at the terrified child.

"Where do you think you're going?" he snarled.

But Bingo snarled louder. Then he jumped and attacked Eli's gun hand. The little girl fled while Bingo struggled with Eli.

"Lennie! Lennie!" Eli cried. Lennie was a very sound sleeper. Finally, Lennie's eyes blinked open. He yawned lazily and stretched. He was completely unaware of the life-and-death struggle that was going on in the trailer.

"I had the craziest dream," he began. Then he finally saw his partner and the dog fighting with one another. Eli had his gun and was trying to shoot Bingo!

Lennie grabbed his own gun and shot it upward through the ceiling. "That's *enough*!" He sounded like a parent who was frustrated by the childish fights between brothers and sisters. "I don't know which one of you started this, but you're both going to get us in big trouble."

He was right about that. For just then, a bullhorn sounded from outside the trailer.

"We know you're in there! Come out with your hands up and nobody will get hurt."

Eli glanced out the window. "Uh-oh. They've got us surrounded."

"We're okay," Lennie assured him. "Why do you think we got hostages?" He opened the closet door. All that was left of the hostages was the tattered ropes that had once held them. Lennie didn't have to be told what had happened to them. He glared at Bingo. "I took you in! And fed you!"

Bingo had no regrets. The Velveeta cheese had been moldy anyway.

* * *

In a motel room far away from the trailer park, the television screen flickered with a news report. The reporter stood in front of a trailer, a tired, but relieved man standing next to him.

". . . And the Thompson family credits this remarkable dog with saving their lives," the reporter said. The camera pulled back to reveal two young girls smothering a dog with hugs and kisses.

"What are your plans now, Mr. Thompson?" the reporter asked.

"We still have a few days vacation left, but we're going back to dog-proof our house so we can give this little fellow the best home he's ever had."

The two girls pulled back a little from the hero dog.

In the motel room, a young boy's jaw dropped.

"Bingooooooo!" Chuckie cried.

At that moment, Bingo reached a paw forward and touched the lens of the camera as if he were reaching out to touch Chuckie. Chuckie put his hand on the television screen, meeting the image of his dog's paw. Nothing would keep them apart!

* * *

The next morning, the station wagon horn honked impatiently in the parking lot of the motel, but nothing was going to keep Chuckie from finishing what he'd started.

He sat at the vanity table in the room, totally oblivious to the broken furniture and smashed mirrors around him. He carefully folded the letter he'd written and put it in an envelope. On the front he wrote:

> Bingo the Dog
> c/o KYAP Television
> Channel 9

and then he wrote the city and state. He didn't have any idea what their address was, but he figured the post office knew where to find KYAP. He licked a stamp, pasted it on, and dashed out of the motel room. There was a mailbox in the parking lot. He slid the letter through the slot and then hugged the mailbox for good luck. It was almost as if he were hugging his beloved dog.

"I haven't forgotten you, pal. Don't give up, fellah. You'll find me."

The horn honked again. Chuckie dashed for the car. As they pulled out of the motel parking lot, they could hear the motel owner yelling.

"Hey! What happened in here? A demolition derby?"

It wasn't surprising he was upset about the condition of the room. Placekickers could make a real mess when they were practicing in a small space.

Dad stepped on the gas. They were out of there.

12

For Bingo, life with the Thompsons was not a bed of roses. It was more a bed of daisies and buttercups and Bingo didn't much like it.

In the first place, the two girls, Cindy and Sandy, couldn't agree on a name. Cindy called him Eugene. Sandy called him Cuddles. It turned Bingo's stomach. What was wrong with good old Bingo for a name?

Worse than that, however, they treated him like a baby or a doll or both. He found himself being forced to sit in a doll carriage, wearing a bunting and a bonnet. That outfit made Lauren's rhinestone tiara and tulle skirt seem like a good idea!

Then, just when Bingo thought it couldn't get any worse, Mr. Thompson came into the girls' room and introduced a dumpy man to Bingo.

"You Bingo?" the man asked.

"Woof!"

The man reached out and handed him some papers. Bingo took them in his mouth.

"It's a subpoena," the man explained, and then he left.

A subpoena? What did that mean?

"It means you're going to testify in court," Mr. Thompson explained.

". . . And do you swear to tell the whole truth and nothing but the truth, so help you God?"

"Woof!"

"Your Honor, I object," said the defense attorney. "This is a court of law, not a kennel!"

"Overruled!" the judge bellowed. "Didn't you ever have a dog when you were a kid? Proceed."

Bingo looked around the courtroom. It seemed like everybody was there. He saw the Thompsons, lots of police officers, and plenty of reporters. He also saw Eli and Lennie. Lennie smiled and waved. Eli glared at him. Bingo glared back.

The prosecutor approached Bingo. "Were you present on the night when the Thompson camper was hijacked by two ruthless armored car thieves who held the family captive until the following morning?"

"*Woof! Woof!*"

"Are those two thieves in this courtroom?"

"*Woof!*"

"Would you please identify them for us?"

Bingo pointed with his paw. He growled for effect.

"Traitor!" Lennie said.

"I'll get you!" Eli threatened. Bingo wasn't afraid, though. He'd done the right thing.

"No further questions, your honor," the prosecutor said. Bingo began to hop down off the witness stand.

"Not so fast there, fleabag," the defense attorney said. "I've got a little cross-examining to do here."

There was a murmur of surprise in the courtroom. Bingo returned to his seat.

"Your honor, could I have the court reporter read back the dog's testimony in response to his whereabouts on the day in question?"

"The court reporter will do so," the judge instructed.

The woman lifted the stream of paper that emerged from her machine and glanced at it carefully. When she found the beginning of Bingo's testimony, she began reading.

"Woof! Woof! Woof! Woof! Grrrr! Woof! Woof!"

"That's what I thought," the defense attorney said. Then he turned to Bingo. "You only indicated you were in the Thompsons' camper and not *why* you were there. Can you tell the court where you were during the armored car robbery earlier that day?"

"Objection, your honor. Irrelevant," the prosecutor said.

"Where are you headed with this, counselor?" the judge asked Eli and Lennie's attorney.

"Your honor, I have witnesses who will testify to seeing this dog near a garbage can just before the robbery."

He went to his table and picked up a baggie with a plaster cast in it. He tossed it to the prosecutor. Then he continued.

"We would also like to introduce exhibits 'Q' and 'R' — a chemical report and paw-print impressions that substantiate the fact that this mutt was at the scene of the crime!"

"Wait just one minute — " The prosecutor tried to interrupt. It didn't work though. The defense attorney just barged right ahead.

"Isn't it true," he said, glaring at Bingo, "that you were the one who robbed the armored car? And didn't you subsequently frame my clients in

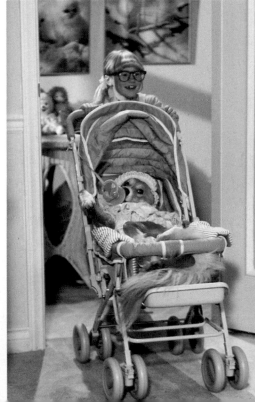

a clever scheme to earn you wealth, respect, and a room of your own?"

There were audible gasps in the courtroom. Bingo was too stunned to bark.

"This is absurd," the prosecutor protested.

"The dog will answer the question," the judge said.

"Don't answer," the prosecutor told Bingo. "You have rights."

"Answer, or I'll throw you in the slammer for contempt of court!" the judge roared.

"What's the matter — cat got your tongue?" the defense attorney taunted.

Bingo was so confused he could only whimper.

"Take him away!" the judge said, smacking his gavel for order in the court.

13

Jail was rough. First, they assigned Bingo a number and took his picture with it. Then he was paw-printed and booked. The desk sergeant took off his collar and put it in an envelope. Alone, Bingo was led to a cell. The slamming door echoed forlornly through the jailhouse. Bingo looked around — ten feet by seven feet, two bunks, a chair and a toilet, and that was it. Well, he discovered, that wasn't quite all that was there. He also had a roommate.

A thin man with thick glasses looked down from the top bunk. His glasses were so thick they made the man look as if he had four eyes.

"Well, this looks like my lucky day," the man said. Bingo wasn't so sure about that.

It wasn't long, however, before Bingo and Foureyes became close friends, bound together by their common misery and the fact that they shared seventy square feet of living space. The best part was that Foureyes had a plan. He'd already begun digging his way out of jail. Bingo was a much better digger than he was.

"Hey, you're really good!" Foureyes said, looking at the growing pile of dirt. Bingo's digging paws were going so fast they were almost invisible. "Have you done this before?" Foureyes asked. If only Bingo could have told him about Duke's place!

Then there was a whistle from one of their neighbors. The guard was coming. Bingo replaced the tiles over the hole. Foureyes dealt the cards.

"Gin!" Foureyes declared, laying down his hand just as the guard got to their cell.

"You got mail," the guard said.

"It's about time," Foureyes said.

"Not you — him," the guard said, pointing to Bingo. He held up the envelope. It was from a motel. It had been sent to a television station and then to the Thompsons. Could it be? Bingo barked eagerly.

"Not now. *After* work," the guard sneered, pocketing the envelope.

When the sixteenth load of laundry was done, Bingo's work was done. The guard gave him the envelope. Bingo handed it to Foureyes to open and read to him. He'd waited long enough. He was really eager.

"All right, all right. I'm opening it," his cell mate said. "Says here:

'Dear Bingo, I'm writing so you'll know I still think of you as my dog and I want you to find me so as we can resume our happy life together. I saw those Thompson girls on the tube and if you ask me they look like real dodo birds.'"

"Woof!"

"*'So I am asking you to blow them off, even if it is a semi-happy home, and pick up my trail, which I knew you were following, because I have faith that you know I am the perfect kid for you because I am lonely and picked on like you.*

"*'Anyway, if you do this and find me, we will finally be happy, which I know you will like. See you soon I hope.*

Your best friend, Chuckie

"*'P.S. I forgot to tell you where I am, which I better do now, because knowing you, you'll sniff this letter and try to retrace its delivery cross-country to where I mailed it from (ha! ha!). Anyway, all you have to do is get yourself to —'*"

Before Foureyes could read another word, the letter was jerked out of his hand.

62

Bingo looked up to see what had happened. What he saw was Eli, holding the letter, and Lennie standing next to him.

"Lie down with dogs and you wake up with fleas," Lennie said to Foureyes.

Bingo's cell mate leapt to his feet, but as soon as he saw that Lennie was approximately twice his size, he backed off a little. "You talking to me?" he asked meekly.

"No!" Eli stormed. "We're talking to that good-for-nothing, backstabbing, double-crossing hair-wad next to you!"

Foureyes was little, but he was tough. "My friend wants his letter," he said insistently.

Lennie didn't move. Foureyes did. In a movement too fast to see, his arm struck out, grabbed the letter and pulled — tearing it in half. He handed the ripped paper to Bingo.

Lennie still held a tattered half. "Come and get it," he said. He pulled out a homemade knife.

Foureyes pulled out a *bigger* homemade knife.

The other inmates in the laundry pulled out homemade knives, too.

Bingo barked like crazy.

"Who's doing all the barking?" demanded a guard.

All the knives disappeared. So did all the mean

looks. By the time the guard reached the group of inmates, the prisoners looked so innocent that they might have been a sewing circle.

"If that's the way you want to play it, get back to your cells."

All the inmates turned to go. The guard dispersed the crowd, but not before Lennie and Eli had the chance to share some thoughts with Bingo.

"You're dog meat, pal," Lennie said.

"It ain't over 'til it's over," Eli added.

14

"It's time!" Foureyes whispered to Bingo in the pitch-black night. Silently, the two of them got out of their bunks and removed the tiles from the floor of their cell. The tunnel was finished. They were busting out of jail.

When they emerged in the prison courtyard, spotlights swept the area, but there was no pattern to them — no indication that anybody had yet noticed that two desperadoes had broken out.

Bingo and Foureyes crawled on their stomachs, heading for the wall, heading for freedom. They had everything planned perfectly. Nothing could go wrong. Could it?

In the tower above the yard, the guard sat attentively — all his attention focused on the magazine he was reading. Then he thought he heard a sound. Yes! His microwave popcorn was done. He took the bag out of the microwave and returned to his magazine article.

Bingo and Foureyes reached the wall. As planned, Foureyes made a stirrup with his hands and helped boost Bingo over the wall. Next, he tied a toilet seat to a length of rope and tossed that over to Bingo. Foureyes tied the rope around his waist. Bingo slid into their cell-made toilet-seat harness and began to pull.

It took all his super-canine strength, tugging hard enough to pull Foureyes up over the twenty-foot wall, but Bingo was driven every inch of the way by his devotion to his cell mate, his intense loyalty, and his need to relieve himself. The nearest bush was twenty feet away — exactly the distance he'd need to go to haul Foureyes to safety. Foureyes practically flew up the wall!

Pretty soon, Foureyes was up and over the wall. They were free. The only trouble was that Foureyes had had a little tangle with the barbed wire on the top of the wall. His face was bleeding. Bingo licked it lovingly.

"Don't worry about me, boy. I just need a little after-shave. Shhhh!" he said.

The two of them looked up at the top of the

wall. Perhaps it was Bingo's sympathetic whimpers, perhaps it was Foureye's shrieking when he hit the barbed wire, but the guard had finally put down his magazine and come to investigate.

They saw him standing behind the parapet above them. He had his gun in his hands and his flashlight in his mouth. He moved his head, and the beam from his flashlight swished around the countryside. Bingo and Foureyes crouched in terror. The beam of the flashlight didn't find them. Eventually, though, the light slipped out of the guard's mouth and clattered noisily to the ground. The last thing they heard was "Drat!" The guard retreated to his magazine and his popcorn. They were truly free.

Foureyes turned to Bingo. He pulled the half of Chuckie's letter — the half without Chuckie's address — from his pocket and tucked it securely into Bingo's collar.

"I hope you know what you're doing," Foureyes said. "The post office isn't much for direct routes. But I guess you'll do all right, you lucky son-of-a-gun. I'll never forget you."

It was a tender moment. Bingo licked Foureyes on the cheek. Foureyes hugged Bingo. They parted ways.

The last Bingo heard was Foureyes singing to himself.

"There was a con who had a dog, and Bingo was his name-o. B-I-N — "

Bang! Bang! The sounds of gunfire broke the night. Bingo and Foureyes ran for their lives.

15

In a house in Green Bay, Wisconsin, Hal Devlin sat in his easy chair, reading the sports section. The headline read:

CAN DEVLIN DO IT?

Kicking Game Key to Packer Play-off Hopes

Dad put down the newspaper and looked at his bare foot, propped on an ottoman.

"What is it, Hal?" Mom asked.

"It's tingling!" Dad said, wiggling his toes. "Like it used to. Remember?" He cradled his foot and stared at it the way a mother gazes lovingly at a newborn baby. "I'd forgotten what it felt like, Natalie." Mom came over to inspect the tingling foot. "The touch — I think it's coming back! I think the old foot is finally waking up!"

Chuckie watched all of this from where he sat in front of the television. It was good news all right because it could only mean one thing as far as Chuckie was concerned.

"Bingo! He's on his way!" Chuckie cried. Chickie knuckled him on the top of his head. Chuckie didn't care. "I knew it! I told you he'd come!"

Chuckie didn't care that nobody believed him.

Bingo had to sniff every truck in the post office yard before he found the one that had The Scent of having carried Chuckie's letter. Now all he had to do was to backtrack that Scent until he found where the letter had been mailed from and he'd be on Chuckie's trail again! He didn't waste a second.

There it was! Bingo was certain he'd found the truck. He was practically home free. He sniffed wildly around the parking lot until he knew which route the truck had used to get in there. The Scent was just a couple of weeks old — nothing at all for a super-scenter like Bingo. He found the trail and he was on his way.

Foureyes hadn't been kidding when he'd said that the post office didn't use direct routes. Bingo didn't mind, though. He was convinced that every step was bringing him closer to Chuckie.

Of course, the ten-foot snow drifts in the Rockies were a little tricky to negotiate, but it was easier than the long swim across the Great Salt Lake. Bingo got very thirsty there. He didn't mind the Grand Canyon, although he was afraid for a minute that he'd lose his balance on the log across a chasm. The scenery was beautiful, though. Death Valley was tough — no question about it. He loped determinedly across the arid desert, driven by his love for Chuckie. The rainstorm in Oregon was torrential, sheets of water driving into his face. He sniffed for The Scent in spite of the weather. The broad plains of Wyoming were beautiful, even in the whiteout blizzard. Bingo didn't care. He didn't need to see. He only had to be able to smell. And smell, he did — until he reached South Dakota, where the snow turned into hail. Bingo slunk under a row of parked cars there, avoiding the golf-ball-sized chunks of ice that fell from the sky.

Bingo was oblivious to the charms of Chicago, ever driven forward, toward Lake Michigan, by The Scent. He picked it up at a dock on the lake. Bingo didn't hesitate. He jumped right into the water. At least he could drink this water — once he was well away from the shore. He didn't even have to get out onto land to get to Lake Huron. He just swam right under the Mackinaw Bridge and in only a few hundred more miles he was in Detroit.

From there, The Scent took him southward by railroad car to Kentucky, home of the Derby, and then due west to Kansas City. Bingo had to sniff a lot there. He got there in the middle of rush hour. The roads were filled with confusing and conflicting scents. But soon he found The Scent, though it was becoming weaker from the passage of time or from total olfactory exhaustion, in other words, nose burnout. It didn't matter to Bingo. Nothing was going to stop him — especially now when he was getting closer. Even the post office had its limits on roundabout routes!

Next stop, the Land of Lincoln: Illinois.

As Bingo closed in on his quarry, he began sniffing every mailbox he saw. He couldn't afford to miss one because he couldn't afford to make a mistake.

He sniffed and sniffed and sniffed, checking out thousands of mailboxes in hundreds of towns and cities in Illinois. Each one might be The One. None of them was. Until . . .

Bingo spotted a rundown motel with a mailbox in the big parking lot. He sniffed. Maybe, he thought. Totally exhausted, but still driven by his love for Chuckie, he took a few tentative steps toward the dented mailbox. The Scent! It was there. Bingo sniffed the mailbox to be sure. He was sure! This was it! A few more steps to the nearby motel room door, where the window was boarded up with plywood.

Chuckie! Chuckie! Chuckie! was all he could think. Weakly, he pawed at the door. After a few seconds, it opened a crack. A woman looked through the screen door.

With his last ounce of energy, Bingo stood up on his haunches and put his paws forward in a begging stance. He whimpered pathetically.

"Awww! It's a cute doggie!" she cried. "And he needs a vet!" Bingo collapsed. "I think we'd better hurry," she said.

16

The vet shook his head solemnly as he prepared for surgery on Bingo. Bingo couldn't figure out what was going on. He was still too exhausted to think clearly.

"You have the olfactory receptors for the transplant?" he asked.

"They're from a Doberman," his assistant said. "It was the best I could do."

"Well, we have no choice. Without a transplant, his sense of smell is shot. He's overworked his own nose and his nasal membrane looks like a worn-out shoe!"

Bingo realized then that he was having a nose transplant!

"Knock him out," the doctor said. "Let's slap

those babies in his schnozz. I just hope we're not too late!"

Bingo hoped so, too.

"Bingooooooo!" Chuckie called down the long hallway of his new school. There was no answer. Chuckie thought he'd heard a familiar bark. One day, he knew Bingo *would* find him! Just not today. Forlornly, he began singing to himself.

"There was a kid who had a dog . . . I know you're here, boy. Say something. Do something! *And Bingo was his name-o! B-I-N —* "

"Do you have a pass, young man?" a shrill voice demanded. It was Mrs. Grimbleby, the scourge of the halls, and better known as The Grim Reaper!

Chuckie gulped. *"You've* got hall duty?"

"Aren't you supposed to be in biology, Chickie?"

"No, I'm Chuckie."

"Don't sass me, young man!"

"But I thought I heard my dog, and — "

"Dog! What dog?" Mrs. Grimbleby demanded, snatching Chuckie by his arm. "When I'm through with you, you're going to beg for more homework!"

Chuckie didn't doubt it for a minute. He

groaned in despair until he heard, "Woof!" It was faint, but it was real. It was Bingo! He shook his arm free from The Grim Reaper.

"Bingo! Bingo!" he cried, certain now that the barking was coming from inside one of the lockers. He ran down the hall, desperately opening every locker as he went. Nothing, no sign of Bingo. The Grim Reaper chased him, grabbing for his arm, trying to stop him, but nothing would stop Chuckie from finding his beloved Bingo!

Finally, he reached the last locker, his last hope. Just as he grabbed the latch, The Grim Reaper grabbed his arm and pulled him away.

"You're in very serious trouble, young man! You'll be twenty-five years old before you're out of detention!"

The door on the locker swung open. There he was. There was Bingo, just as he remembered him, except for one thing. There, in the middle of his face, where Bingo's fuzzy lovable nose ought to be, was the nose of a Doberman pinscher.

"Aaaaaaahhhhhh!" Chuckie screamed. He sat bolt upright in bed, covered with sweat and shaking with fear.

"Are you all right, dear?" his mother asked, turning on the light as she came into Chuckie's room. She sat on his bed and hugged him.

Chuckie looked around to reassure himself. "It was a nightmare, that's all," he said.

In a motel room far away, the vet unwound the bandages from Bingo's nose.

"He'll need plenty of tactile stimulation," the vet told Bunny, the woman who had found Bingo. "That means patting and stroking."

Bingo thought he'd enjoy that. He always liked being patted.

Finally, the last of the bandages was off. Bunny looked at him and gasped. Then she smiled. "Just kidding," she said. Some joke, he thought.

Bunny turned the chair so Bingo could see himself in the mirror. It was Bingo, pure Bingo and it looked great. He barked cheerfully.

"Let's see how the old sniffer's working," the vet said. He took out a deck of cards and let Bingo sniff the queen of spades. Then he took two other cards and put the three together face down. He switched the three cards around deftly, talking as he went.

"Watch the queen! She moves, she grooves, she's here, she's there, she's nowhere! Find the queen, Bingo!"

He sniffed the backs of the cards and put his paw on the familiar scent. The vet turned it over. Bingo was right.

"I could have sworn it was the card on the left," Bunny said.

"That's because you're using your eyes, not your nose," the vet said.

"That's fantastic!"

Bingo thought it was fantastic, too. He thought it meant he could continue following The Scent. Bunny had something else in mind.

As soon as the vet was gone, Bingo and Bunny went in search of a game of three-card monte, just like the vet had been playing. With a twenty-dollar bet on every hand, Bingo and Bunny cleaned up in a matter of minutes.

"Three hundred and twenty bucks!" Bunny shouted gleefully when they returned to the motel.

Bingo wasn't gleeful. He just stared out the window.

"You want to play ball?" Bunny asked. Bingo shook his head. "How about a chew stick? You want one?" He didn't move. "A squeaky toy? Lots of fun!" She squeezed a rubber bone and tossed it toward Bingo. He stared at it sadly.

"What's the matter? Day after day, all you do

is look out that window." Bingo looked out the window. Bunny went on. "I read the letter. What was left of it, anyway," she said. "You came here looking for Chuckie, didn't you? I guess if you've got to go, you've got to go."

Bingo's ears perked up, and he licked Bunny's face joyously.

Bunny took Bingo to the bus station. "The motel man said they went to Green Bay. The bus will get you there, but then you're on your own. Find your little boy and start your life again. I'll be fine, all by myself." She sniffed a tear back. "I've knitted a little something for you," she said.

She opened a shoebox and took out a long pink knitted tube. Bingo looked at it in surprise. "It's a tail warmer," she explained. "They've got mean winters in Green Bay. And I've packed you some other travel goodies — dog biscuits, a puzzle, magazines, cold cream and jelly sandwiches, your favorite . . ."

Bingo was nearly moved to tears. Then they heard the announcement of the bus for Green Bay. Bunny carried him to the bus and put him on it. He hung out the window by his seat for a final good-bye. "You crazy mutt! I guess I just didn't know what real love was until you came along. You saved me, Bingo!"

The bus' engine roared to life.

"My whole life's still ahead of me!" Bunny went on. "Maybe I can do volunteer work, or get a degree in nursing, or even therapy . . ."

Bingo barked his final good-bye to Bunny, a true friend.

17

The next day, at another bus stop, two men and a bloodhound searched the garbage for signs of Bingo. The bloodhound rooted through the pile of trash and emerged, barking excitedly, pushing a shoebox with his snout.

Eli lifted the lid of the discarded shoebox. He found the remains of some dog biscuits, a crumpled magazine, a weird knitted tube thing, and a plastic sandwich bag with only the crusts of a sandwich remaining. Eli sniffed.

"Cold cream and jelly," he told Lennie.

"Well at least *he's* eating something! I'm starved!" Lennie said.

"Shut up!" Eli reminded him. "We're getting warmer."

"Darn it, Eli, I didn't bust out of the joint to

spend the rest of my life tracking that mutt. Forget the dog!"

Eli grabbed Lennie by the collar. "Forget! If I put you behind bars, would you forget?" Lennie shook his head. "No, you'd never forget! Never! Besides, if word gets out we let a *dog* get away with it, we're finished — humiliated! We're professionals and we've got a score to settle. Are you with me or not?"

Lennie nodded his head meekly.

The bus drew to a stop in Green Bay. Bingo hopped off and began his search for Chuckie. He sniffed wildly in the bus station, but there was no sign of The Scent. Bingo knew the Devlins had arrived by car. He didn't expect to find a trail in the bus station. So, he did the next most logical thing: He looked in the phone book.

There he found a listing for H. Devlin on Filbert Court. A check of the city map posted by the entrance to the bus station gave Bingo all the information he needed. The last piece of the puzzle was slipping into place. It was just a matter of minutes before reunion time with Chuckie. Confidently, he trotted out of the bus station.

A couple of miles later he found the Devlins. He recognized them when he was still a few hundred yards away. Dad was on the porch of the Devlins' modest frame house, ready to leave for practice. Mom handed him a bag of sports gear. Then Bingo saw Chuckie. He was nearby, walking on the other side of a hedge. He waved good-bye to his father.

Bingo's feet couldn't carry him fast enough. This was it — the moment he'd been waiting and working for! He was about to be back together again with Chuckie. He leaped and bounded toward the hedge until —

Bingo couldn't believe his eyes. It was Chuckie all right. But he was walking with another dog! A hundred thoughts entered Bingo's mind, none of them good. He was overwhelmed with a sadness and a feeling of loss. He'd taken too long to find Chuckie. Chuckie couldn't wait for him anymore. Chuckie had gotten another dog. There would be no more room for Bingo in Chuckie's heart.

Bingo couldn't even bring himself to bark. He whimpered instead. His head dropped. His tail drooped. He turned and walked away slowly. His life had no more meaning.

Chuckie finished walking Frisker. He took the little dog up onto Mrs. Wallaby's porch to return him home. Frisker wasn't bad, but he wasn't any Bingo.

"We're home, Mrs. Wallaby," Chuckie called through the screen door.

Mrs. Wallaby appeared. She took Frisker's leash and handed Chuckie a dollar. "It's so nice of you to walk him for me," Mrs. Wallaby said, as she always did.

"He's a good dog," Chuckie told her. "Of course, he's not like Bingo, but then, no dog is."

Mrs. Wallaby nodded sweetly. She didn't have the faintest idea what Chuckie was talking about.

Each step took Bingo farther from Chuckie. Each step made him sadder. He wandered forlornly, not knowing where he was going, not caring either.

His heart was very heavy, and his stomach was empty. Bingo paused at the glass front of a place called Vic's Café and watched a man eat a hearty meal. The children with him left a lot of food on their plates. Vic gave them doggie bags. That made Bingo think more about his stomach than his heart and it gave him an idea. He went around to the back of the café to see if he could dig up a doggie bag for himself.

He was well into his second course when a large

hand grabbed his collar and yanked him away from the overturned garbage can.

"You're new here, aren't you?" the man said, looking Bingo straight in the eye. Bingo was too stunned to nod. "Well, I don't care how pathetic you are, if you want food from me, you've got to earn your keep."

Before Bingo could say anything, he found himself in the kitchen, wearing an apron, standing next to a teenage boy named Dave, and looking at an enormous pile of dirty dishes.

"I'll have more when you finish with these. Dave, here, will show you the ropes." Then Vic turned to Dave. "Stay on your toes. This mutt looks ambitious."

18

Eli finished nailing another poster onto another telephone pole. The poster showed a crude drawing of Bingo — Eli had spent some time in prison graphics shops during his career — and offered a $500 reward to anyone who would help them find Bingo.

Lennie was uncomfortable about offering a big reward. "If we're going to dole money out, why don't we send something in to protect the ozone layer?"

"That wouldn't get us the dog back, now would it?" Eli said.

"I'm just saying five hundred bucks is a lot for a reward," Lennie said.

"Who says we're going to pay up? We're scum,

Lennie. We don't have to pay up. Now, quit your bellyaching. We've got ground to cover."

The first person who saw the poster was Chuckie. He spotted it on the way to school.

"Bingo! I knew it!" he said, almost whispering with excitement. Then he read the rest of the poster. "If you have any information leading to our dog Bingo contact room 12 at the Highway Motor Inn. Ask for Mr. Smith."

Chuckie ripped the poster off the phone pole and rode his bike as fast as he could. He wouldn't call the number; he'd go there, first thing, as soon as school was out.

There was a knock at the motel room door. Lennie opened the door. He saw a teenager with dishpan hands. It was Dave from Vic's Café.

"Yeah? What do you want, pal?" Lennie asked.

"Are you Mr. Smith?" Dave asked.

Lennie wasn't too bright. He'd already forgotten that Mr. Smith was the name they'd put on the poster. He turned to Eli. "Hey, Eli, is there a Mr. Smith here?"

He was answered by a sharp jab in the ribs from Eli's elbow. That jogged his memory.

"We're Mr. Smith," Eli said.

Dave knew phonies when he saw them, but he also knew $500 would get him out of washing a lot of dishes. He didn't care what these guys were up to.

"Well, I think the dog you're looking for is working at Vic's Café as the *assistant* dishwasher."

"You sure?" Eli demanded.

"He ain't been promoted *yet*," Dave said.

Eli and Lennie brushed past Dave, running for their stolen car. They paused only long enough to hand Dave a leash holding Ol' Blue the bloodhound.

"Hey! What about my reward?" Dave demanded, yelling to be heard over the roar of the car's engine.

Lennie lowered the window as he drove away, calling back to Dave, "Sell Ol' Blue!"

Dave was left alone in the parking lot. He was fuming mad.

That was when Chuckie arrived. He was pedaling his bike furiously and was nearly out of breath. He drew to a stop by Dave.

"What's going on here?" Chuckie asked.

"Want to buy a dog?" Dave countered.

* * *

Vic was pleased with his new employee.

"You're a hard worker, Bingo. I like that. You be here at six tomorrow and we'll talk more about career opportunities in the food service industry."

Bingo took the food Vic offered him and left the café for the day. But his day wasn't over yet — not by a long shot.

As soon as he stepped out the back door, Bingo found himself looking at a very familiar menacing face. It was Lennie.

"Well, if it ain't Mr. Whole-truth-and-nothing-but-the-truth-flea-carrying-turncoat-snitch."

Eli was behind him and he had a rope to put around Bingo's neck. Bingo was trapped!

Chuckie skidded into the alley on his bicycle. He sized up the situation immediately.

"Let go of my dog, you jerk!" he screamed.

That just made Lennie and Eli run away with Bingo faster, so Chuckie took direct action: He rammed right into them!

For a few seconds, there was a mess of arms, legs, and bicycle, all flailing wildly. Out of it emerged Bingo, dragging a rope around his neck, but no captor's hand held him.

"Run, Bingo! Run!" Chuckie shrieked.

Bingo knew when he and Chuckie were in over

their heads. They needed help and Bingo was the one who could get it.

The last thing Chuckie saw before Eli and Lennie hustled him into their stolen car was the sight of Bingo running for freedom — and help.

19

Lennie was behind the wheel. Eli sat at the window. Chuckie was squeezed — very squeezed — in between them.

"I'm losing patience, boy. He's your dog. Now you're going to tell us where he is."

Chuckie tried to sound tough. "How am I supposed to know? ESP?"

Eli glared. "Think real hard, kid, or it's going to cost you." Eli puffed on a cigar. The end of it glowed a fiery red. Eli held the cigar very close to Chuckie's face.

Chuckie had been brought up to believe that a good offense was the best defense. He tried.

"Y-y-y-you don't s-s-s-scare me." He gulped. "When my dad gets wind of this, he'll beat the hair off you."

"Yeah? Him and who else?" Lennie sneered.

Chuckie played his trump card. "How about the offensive line of the Green Bay Packers?"

"What is he? President of the booster club?" Eli asked.

"Try Hal Devlin," Chuckie said.

"Devlin? The placekicker?" Chuckie nodded proudly. "He stunk up the stadium in Denver. Cost me some big dollars."

"Well, he's ten for ten with Green Bay and we're going to make the play-offs after we hammer Detroit!" Chuckie said confidently.

"What is this? *NFL Today*?" Lennie asked.

"Wait a second!" Eli said. He'd just gotten a bright idea. Chuckie had the feeling he wasn't going to like it. "How would you like to score some *real* money?"

"What about the dog? We're after the *dog*," Lennie reminded him.

"Trust me on this one, Lennie. We are going to make a bundle! This kid is our passport to Fat City. Look at him. What do you see?"

Lennie glanced at Chuckie sideways. "A kid. So what?" he said.

"That's what's wrong with you, Lennie. This isn't a kid. This is a winning lottery ticket with hair! We've been dealt a royal flush and you're too busy counting the spots on the cards to play the hand!"

Chuckie didn't like the sound of it. Neither did Lennie.

"But the dog," Lennie began.

"Forget the dog! If we're smart enough, we can make enough to hire a battalion of dog catchers!"

20

What Eli and Lennie didn't know as they drove their car through the streets of Green Bay, was that the very dog they were stalking was also driving through the streets of Green Bay — on top of their car!

The blue Chevy pulled to a halt by an old abandoned warehouse. Bingo scampered silently to a hiding place behind a stack of empty crates. He watched every move, waiting for the right moment.

Bingo sniffed around every inch of the warehouse. He wanted to be sure he knew every way in and out before he attempted a rescue or ran for help. He couldn't afford to make a mistake. He just couldn't let Chuckie down.

Bingo climbed up onto a pile of tires and peeked inside the warehouse through a dusty window.

There he saw Chuckie. He was tied to a chair. He was gagged. His Green Bay Packers hat was knocked crooked. He looked frightened.

Bingo thought he spotted a way in. He dashed down the pile of tires and headed straight for it. Before he got there, Lennie and Eli entered the room where Chuckie was. Bingo stopped and watched. Lennie and Eli were arguing.

"You don't understand because you're a technocrat," Eli said to Lennie. Lennie thought that sounded like an insult. "You build devices. You work with your hands. I, on the other hand, am a visionary. I work with my mouth. Now, I've got to find a phone and get the ball rolling before kickoff."

"Yeah, but Eli — is it a good idea to gamble everything we have on *one* game?"

Eli looked exasperated. "Lennie, it isn't gambling when you mark the deck. You worry about the kid and rigging the device."

With that Eli left, slamming the door behind him.

Bingo didn't like the sound of any of this. He was so upset he fogged up the glass and couldn't see very well. He used his paw to clear a peephole. When he looked again, he had to blink to be sure he'd seen it right. Lennie was packing thirty sticks of dynamite into a suitcase and had a timing device in his hands. He was also talking to himself.

"If this plan doesn't work, the next bomb will be wired to Eli's shorts — *partner*!"

Lennie had a remote controller that looked like a garage door opener. None of this looked like good news to Bingo.

When Lennie took the device to another room in the warehouse, Bingo sprang into the room where Chuckie was tied up.

"Biwo, wa aw woo ooinh ee?" Chuckie asked. The gag made it pretty hard to understand, but Bingo was clever. He knew that Chuckie was saying, "Bingo, what are you doing here?"

That was when Bingo remembered that Chuckie told him to go for help, not to be a help. He looked down at the floor, embarrassed.

"You've got to get help. Go to my house. Get somebody. Now!" Chuckie said as clearly as he could. Bingo hesitated. "Now!" Chuckie hissed. Bingo knew Chuckie was right. He bolted for a hole in the wall and left, but not before he knocked over a ladder.

"What's going on in here?" Lennie yowled from the next room.

Chuckie's mind raced. He had to come up with

some sort of excuse for a noise. He sang, through the gag.

" 'Ere wah a fahmah ha a og, anh Biwo wah hi am-o!"

"Ah, shut up! I hate that song!" Lennie yelled. Chuckie stopped singing.

21

Mom was all ready for her football party. Every surface in the house was covered with something that said Green Bay or Packers, or both. A green-and-gold helmet was filled with green and gold popcorn. The television was tuned and ready for the game to begin.

The doorbell rang. Mom thought it was the first guests. It wasn't. It was just a scraggly dog. He was jumping up and down and barking.

"Who are you?"

"Woof! Woof!"

"We don't want any. Now get out of here. Shoo! Shoo!" She slammed the door.

Later, right after the national anthem, the doorbell rang again. This time, Mom sent Chickie to answer it.

Chickie opened the door. It was a scraggly dog.

He was jumping up and down and barking, though it wasn't easy to bark because he had a Green Bay Packers hat in his mouth.

"Wooh! Wooh!"

Chickie took the hat. "Where did you get this?" Chickie asked. Bingo barked. "Just a minute," Chickie said. He took the hat and slammed the door in Bingo's face. He returned to the living room.

"Who was it?" Mom asked.

"Some dog with a hat. It looks like Chuckie's," Chickie said, handing the hat to Mom. She added it to the centerpiece on the table.

"Don't be silly," she said, crimping the crepe paper. "Do you know how many Packer caps there are in this town?"

Chickie shrugged. He returned to the front door to chase the dog away.

The phone rang. Mom answered it. She had trouble understanding the man at the other end of the line, though. His voice was muffled and the fact that the kitchen doorbell was buzzing didn't help.

"Chickieeeee!" she shouted, and gestured to the door. Then she spoke into the phone. "Could you enunciate a little more clearly? I'm having difficulty understanding . . . you've got my what?"

Chickie was tired of being a doorman, especially for a dog who seemed to be a used clothing salesman. This time he had a Green Bay Packers shirt in his mouth. Chickie threatened the mutt. "You again? Get out of here before I call animal control!" He threw a magazine at the mutt. The dog dodged the magazine, dropped the shirt, and ran.

Satisfied that he'd gotten rid of the dog, he went into the house. His mother was sitting on a stool, holding the telephone in her hand. She didn't look at all well.

"What's wrong, Mom? You look like you've seen a ghost."

"Who was at the door?"

"That dumb dog again."

Mom dropped the phone on the floor and ran to the door. "Where is he?" she asked.

"I chased him off," Chickie said proudly.

"You've got to find him!"

"Why?"

"Someone's got Chuckie! That dog may know where he is!"

Hal Devlin had time for one more practice kick before the game began. It was a beauty, just like every one he'd kicked since joining Green Bay. He was ten for ten now. Who knew where he'd be by the end of the season? His kicks could even take him to the Super Bowl!

"It's for you," his coach said. Dad looked at him oddly, but the coach took off his earphones and gave them to Dad.

"Hal?" Mom said over the phone. "They've got Chuckie! He's been kidnapped! They said that if we wanted to see him alive again — "

"Pay them! Understand? We'll pay anything!" Dad said.

"It's not exactly that kind of ransom," Mom said. "They want, um, uh. They want — "

Dad didn't have time for *ums* and *uhs*. "Tell me!"

Mom blurted it out. "They want you to miss all your field goals!"

"What?"

"Don't make any field goals against the Tigers," she repeated.

"Lions," he said, correcting her.

"Well, Detroit, whatever!"

"Calm down. It won't do any good to panic. Did they say anything about extra points?"

"No."

"Good. Now call the police and — "

"They said no police. They're serious, Hal."

"How can you be sure?" Dad asked.

"A dog dropped off some of Chuckie's clothing. Chickie's trying to track him down. But Hal — "

All around Dad, his teammates were getting ready for the game, butting helmets, slapping shoulder pads. It made it hard to hear and hard to talk. "Look, I've got to go. Do what you think is best. It's probably just a hoax — "

"Chuckie's our son!" Mom cried out.

Dad could hear that all right, but he couldn't do anything about it. "I've got to go," he repeated. He took off the earphones and handed them back to the coach.

"Everything okay, Devlin?" the coach asked.

Dad lied. "Sure coach. Just a pep talk from the wife."

"That's the ticket," the coach said, patting him on the rear.

Then Dad remembered Chuckie's gift. He was wearing the leather belt. "Tell me, coach. What's more important to you, football or family?" Dad asked, teeing up the ball for a final practice kick.

The coach looked at him quizzically. "You kidding? Football's my life!" he said.

"That's what I thought," Dad said. He took five running steps and kicked the football. It hooked sharply to the left and soared into the crowd, totally missing the practice net.

22

Eli and Lennie huddled over a portable radio in the office of the warehouse. They were listening intently and it was all good news.

". . . and with less than a minute to go in the third quarter, Devlin will try a thirty-two yard field goal that could put the Packers ahead. There's the snap. The kick's up . . . and it's wide. No good! Devlin's second miss from inside the thirty-five yard line and this game is *still* scoreless!"

Eli and Lennie slapped high fives. Everything was working smoothly.

Thump!

"What was that?"

Lennie shrugged. Eli snapped off the radio, Lennie grabbed a flashlight. They went to investigate.

Chuckie was there, tied up safe and sound. His hat was missing and so was his shirt, but he was there and that was what was important. He was barefoot. One of his sneakers lay nearby. The other was nowhere to be seen.

High above Eli and Lennie, Bingo was perched on the rafter of the warehouse. He had Chuckie's other sneaker next to him, carefully balanced. At just the right instant, Bingo nudged the shoe. It tumbled gracefully through the air and landed — *thump!* — next to Eli.

Eli spun around and saw the shoe. Carefully, he pointed the flashlight upwards, into the dark rafters above. He gasped.

Bingo leapt! He practically flew down and landed directly on Eli. He began growling, barking, and biting. Eli didn't like it at all.

"Lennie, get him off me! Off!"

The two thugs began fighting the mutt, but Bingo was fighting mean. He took a bite out of the seat of Eli's pants.

"Yeooooo!!!!" Eli howled.

The fighting went on and they all made so much noise that they never heard Chickie Devlin, still searching for Bingo and Chuckie. He saw everything and he knew just what he had to do. He ran for help.

* * *

"Mom! I found him!" he shrieked, running up onto his porch and bursting into the living room.

"Found who?" Mom asked. She'd been watching the game and she was so upset about what was happening with Dad's kicking that she'd forgotten the reason for it all.

"Chuckie! They've got him in a warehouse with a bomb and — "

"Shhhhhhh."

They both stared at the television set. ". . . and the kick is — wide left! Still no score going into the final quarter. Looks to me like Devlin's a little quick on the trigger. . . ."

"Mo-ther! I found Chuckie!" Chickie said, jumping in front of the television set.

"Oh, my! Where?"

"Some old warehouse. We've got to call the police. Now!"

"We can't do that!"

"We've got no choice!"

"You're genuinely concerned about your brother, aren't you?" Mom asked.

Chickie shrugged. "Well, with him gone, I figure I'd have to take twice as much heat from you and Dad," he reasoned.

Mom reached for the phone.

23

Bingo tugged at the rope that went around his neck and tied him to Chuckie's chair, but it was no use. They were trapped in the warehouse. They were at the mercy of Eli and Lennie and that pair didn't have much mercy at all.

Lennie was putting the finishing touches on the bomb.

"Is this thing ready? I want to push the button," Eli said, glaring at Bingo. He still hurt from the bite Bingo took out of his rear end.

"Hey, I'm the technocrat," Lennie said. "I want to push the button!" He held up the remote controller and talked as if he were advertising it on television. "It's carry-on size, but it packs enough wallop to level a city block. And we can trigger the timer from miles away!" He was very proud of his work.

Eli had just one thing to add to that. He went nose-to-nose with Bingo and began singing.

"There was a crook that had a bomb, and . . . KABLOOEY!" With that, Eli blew a puff of smoke from his cigar into Bingo's face. Bingo coughed and sputtered. Eli tossed the cigar off into the dark recesses of the warehouse. It landed on a pile of old cardboard boxes.

"Come on, Lennie, let's get out of here," he said.

Lennie made a final check of his bomb and the two of them made a dash for their car. They were in such a hurry that they never noticed the curls of smoke coming up out of the pile of boxes where Eli's cigar had landed. All they wanted was to collect on their bets.

They turned on the radio as soon as the car's engine started. They pulled out of the warehouse parking lot. Eli put the pedal to the metal and turned up the Packer game. Lennie fiddled with the remote.

". . . *and the referee starts the clock again on this still scoreless game with four minutes left.*"
Click!

Lennie activated the remote. Nearby garage doors flew open obediently. Back in the warehouse, the timer began its countdown. Three minutes and fifty-nine seconds.

"But wait. The Packers call for a time-out. They'll have the ball as play resumes."

Click! The open garage doors closed. The bomb timer stopped.

"Enough's enough. Stop playing around with that!" Eli snapped.

"Shut up and drive," Lennie said. "It's time I had a little fun for a change!"

Not far away Chickie and Mom rode in the sheriff's car. They listened to the game, too.

"Can't you go any faster?" Chickie said urgently.

"You want me to blow the engine of my car?" the sheriff asked.

"You want my old man to miss another field goal?" Chickie asked.

The sheriff stepped on the accelerator.

Meanwhile, back at the warehouse, big trouble was brewing. The smoldering smoke from the old cardboard boxes was becoming smoldering flame. Chuckie and Bingo both knew that the place was so old and dry that it could explode more violently from the flames than from the bomb. There wasn't a minute to waste.

Bingo used his super-canine strength to chew

through the ropes and soon had freed himself. He began to go to work on Chuckie's bonds.

"It's no use, Bingo," Chuckie said. He looked around for something — some ray of hope. Then he saw it. He spotted a fire alarm box. If only Bingo could sound the alarm. But of course he could. Bingo could do anything!

"Bingo!" Chuckie said excitedly. "Try to break the fire alarm. It's over there, boy!"

Bingo looked where Chuckie was pointing with his gaze. He would do anything for Chuckie — well, almost anything.

There were stacks of abandoned crates, each higher than the one in front of it. It was almost like a flight of stairs leading up to the fire alarm. It would be easy, except for one thing. The crates were already smoldering and the acrid smoke and small flames ignited Bingo's own, painful memories.

"Well, go on!" Chuckie urged him. "Climb the equipment. Jump over those crates there and break the glass. You can do it, Bingo! You've got to do it!"

Bingo hesitated. He tried to make his mind a blank and force the memories away. He climbed to the first level. Flames licked at his heels. He scrambled up to escape them.

"That's it, Bingo!" Chuckie called weakly from below. "Jump the crates. Break the glass. Go for it!" Chuckie waited to hear the sound of breaking glass, but all he heard was the crackle of the growing fire. He squinted to see through the thickening smoke. Bingo was standing absolutely still! "What's wrong, boy?"

There was no way Chuckie could know, no way Bingo could tell him, but Bingo couldn't hide his memories anymore. There it was, as clear as the day it had happened. Flames engulfed the pet store. Bingo's mother perished, along with hundreds of other innocent pets. The cemetery, the sadness, the endless search for happiness. Tears filled the mutt's eyes. Terror filled his heart.

The dog looked again at Chuckie. He was young, loving, and trusting — everything Bingo had been searching for.

"Bingo!" Chuckie called to the dog. It was his last word before he passed out from smoke inhalation. Bingo knew it might be the last word he ever spoke, unless . . .

Yes! He *could* do it! Bingo growled to give himself confidence and then, before he could change his mind, he turned and dashed the last few steps to the top of the pile. He aimed for the fire alarm and, with all his strength and determination, he took a flying leap at the glass. . . .

Meanwhile, the blue Chevy containing Eli and Lennie careened through Green Bay, the radio blaring over the sound of angry horns.

"And the Packers stop the clock again with forty seconds remaining . . ."

Click! Lennie flipped the switch on the remote. Garage doors closed. The bomb timer, now miles away, stopped.

Eli zoomed around a corner and found himself face-to-face with six police cars. They were trapped!

"And Devlin is coming onto the field to attempt a fifty-four yarder . . ."

"What are you doing with that remote?"

"You're not the boss of me," Lennie snapped back. *Click! Click! Click! Click!* He sang a little song as he played with the remote. "Now he's hamburger, now he's not!"

The sheriff grabbed his megaphone and turned it on. He crouched behind the open door of his black-and-white. "Let the boy go and nobody'll get hurt!" the sheriff called out.

Down the alleyway, Eli called back. "Make sure Devlin misses this field goal and the kid'll stay safe and sound!"

"Let me think about it," the sheriff told the kidnappers.

Mom was next to him. She grabbed his arm and gave him a piece of her mind. "Think about it! What's to think about? What about my boy?"

The sheriff reached for his radio. "Dispatch," he said, speaking into the machine. "Patch me through to the Silverdome in Detroit. It's a major emergency."

"What are you doing?" Mom asked.

"First things, first," the sheriff said.

While they waited for the call to be placed, everybody could hear the announcers from the stadium.

"And now Detroit has called another time-out. They want Devlin to think about this kick. And in the meantime, he's been called to the sidelines. This is very unusual, folks. The coach has called him over. Now he's giving him his earphones. What do you think he's doing, Buck? Calling out for pizza? Heh, heh."

"Hello?" Dad's voice came over the police radio.

"Mr. Devlin, this is Sheriff Conally calling from Green Bay. We've got your son and everything is going to be okay, so go out there and nail this field goal for Chuckie!"

"You bet!" Dad said excitedly. Then, before Mom had a chance to tell him that the sheriff wasn't exactly being truthful, the sheriff cut off the connection.

"Well, if he was calling out for a pizza, he must have just won a free one because, did you see that, Buck? He actually kissed the coach!"

Mom wanted to give the sheriff a piece of her mind. She began by giving him a taste of her fist. She pummeled him! The deputies pulled her off.

"Come on, lady. A lot of us have money on this game. Besides, I think these clowns are bluffing."

"Time's running out, sheriff!" Eli yelled.

"Okay, okay, but first I want to see the kid!" the sheriff said over the megaphone.

"He's not here," Eli said.

"Where *is* he?" Sheriff Conally asked.

24

Chuckie was lying on the floor of the warehouse in a puddle of water, surrounded by firemen. He opened his eyes weakly. He was vaguely aware of his own discomfort. He was mostly aware of Bingo's insistent barking. The first words he heard were spoken by one of the firemen.

"What's with the dog?" the man asked.

"Forget the dog. Call the paramedics!" another fireman said.

Then Chuckie understood. He tried to sit up. He coughed. He sputtered. He just had to tell them!

"Wait!" he whispered hoarsely. "A bomb! There's a bomb in the suitcase over there. That's what he's barking about."

The first fireman dashed over to Bingo and turned over the bin that held the dog's attention.

Out spilled two dozen identical suitcases!

"This was a suitcase factory, kid! Which one is it?"

"Forget the paramedics, call the bomb squad!"

Then everything became clear to Chuckie, and none of it looked good at all. "There's no time to get the bomb squad here — they can blow it from anywhere!" There was only one answer to this problem. His name was Bingo. "You've got to find it, boy!" Chuckie said. Bingo didn't seem to like the idea very much. He looked very doubtful. "You want to see us splattered, Bingo?" Chuckie asked. Bingo knew when he had to act. This was it. He used his fine-tuned sniffer and went to work. In a matter of seconds, he had the one. He barked and pawed at it.

"You sure, Bingo?" Chuckie asked.

"Woof!" Bingo barked disgustedly.

"Okay, okay, just get rid of it," Chuckie said.

Bingo picked up the heavy suitcase by the handle and dragged it toward the door of the warehouse.

Meanwhile, back at the police blockade . . .

" *. . . so to break this deadlock, Devlin's going to have to beat his personal best of fifty-three yards,"* the sportscaster said. *"But with only forty* *seconds to go, the Packers have no choice. It's their last chance. Devlin's ready. He's looking confident. The snap. The kick is up . . ."*

In the Silverdome Stadium, Hal Devlin watched his first serious attempt of the afternoon. Chuckie was safe and all was well with the world. Or was it? The football soared high into the air, tumbling end over end. All over the world, Green Bay Packer fans held their breath.

In a field in Green Bay, Bingo ran as fast as his legs could carry him, desperate to keep Chuckie from harm's way. He could run all right, but would it be enough?

In a beat-up Chevy station wagon on a side street in Green Bay, Lennie toyed nervously with the remote controller. "Now he's hamburger, now he's not," he muttered under his breath. Garage doors closed. The clock timer stopped.

"And he missed it! The game is still tied!" the announcer said through clenched teeth.

"Hey, Eli! It worked!" Lennie said, elated.

The sheriff wasn't quite so happy. "You dirty, stinkin' . . ." he muttered. He was talking to Hal Devlin who couldn't hear him because he was hundreds of miles away. Frustrated, the sheriff reached for his rifle.

"Sheriff, no!" Mom said.

She wasn't in time, though. The sheriff pulled the trigger of his shotgun, sending a blast toward the Chevy. Most of the shot went wild. Some of it hit Lennie's hand.

"Yeooowww!" Lennie shrieked and tossed the remote controller out the window of the Chevy. It landed on a sidewalk nearby.

Click!

Garage doors opened.

Chuckie stood in the doorway of the warehouse, watching, but he couldn't see any sign of Bingo. All he saw was a huge explosion in the field where Bingo had gone.

"Bingoooooo!" Chuckie screamed. Then he fainted.

25

Chuckie heard muffled voices around him, people standing over him, and saw bright lights above. A hospital public address system purred the names of doctors. Nearby monitors beeped.

He blinked his eyes. Someone was standing right there.

"Hey, partner. It's your old man," he said.

"Dad?"

"You'd be very proud of your father," Mom said. "He kicked a fifty-two-yarder in overtime to win the game."

Chuckie smiled. He *was* proud of his father.

"Well, it was nothing," Dad said. "Nothing compared to what Chuckie did. That was quite a gesture, son — donating your kidney to a dog. Kind of dumb, but very generous of you."

It all came back then. The explosion, the ambulance, the dire word about Bingo . . .

Chickie said it best, though. "That's not just any dog, Dad. Bingo's a real hero!"

"Chickie's right, Hal," Mom said. "Bingo saved Chuckie's life. Don't scold our son for trying to give a little something back."

Dad smiled bashfully. "I'm sorry. A guy like me can't change overnight, you know." He brushed Chuckie's hair affectionately. "But with a little bit of *luck* . . ." Everybody laughed.

Then Chuckie spoke the words he'd been afraid to ask. "How is Bingo?"

The vet stepped forward. "It's touch and go," he said. "The blast blew a lot of fuzz off him, but thank goodness the bomb was in a tough suitcase or there wouldn't have been anything to transplant your kidney into."

"Can I see him?"

"I reckon you can, son," Dad said. Dad helped Chuckie get into a wheelchair and pushed him down the hall in the hospital to Bingo's room. Bingo was there, lying still on a bed under an oxygen tent. He had tubes coming and going from everywhere. Monitors clicked and beeped efficiently.

Bingo wasn't alone, however. He was completely surrounded by dozens of people standing in his room. Chuckie knew some of them, like Dave from Vic's Café, the Thompsons and Duke and the waitress from the hot dog restaurant. Others were complete strangers to him. They all had at least one thing in common, though. They *all* had flowers, balloons, and get-well cards in their hands. Even Eli and Lennie were there — in handcuffs. Others introduced themselves to Chuckie. There was the judge and the attorneys from the trial; Bingo's cell mate, Foureyes; Steve and Ginger, his owners from the circus; Bunny; Vic; and lots of others.

"They all heard Bingo's story on the nightly news and wanted to pay their respects and to wish him well," Mom explained.

Chuckie made his way over to Bingo's bed. Some of Bingo's friends spoke to him as he went.

"Hope your dog doesn't die," Eli said. Chuckie wasn't sure he really meant it, but Lennie crossed his fingers for good luck. Maybe he did mean it.

"Carrot stick, son?" Duke offered. His apron had a sign that said DUKE'S VEGETARIAN RES-TAURANT. Chuckie thought that was a good idea.

There, standing next to Bingo's bed, was a man wearing denim overalls and a cap that read STAMPER SEED & FEED. Chuckie couldn't imagine what he was doing there and he was even more surprised when the man spoke to him.

"He's yours now, boy. Take good care of him." The man stepped away from Bingo's bed.

"Who are you?" Chuckie asked.

"Bingo's old master," the man said.

"Who?"

The man started to walk out, but changed his mind. "You know," he said. Then he began singing quietly.

"There was a farmer had a dog, and Bingo was his name-o . . ."

"*That* farmer?" Chuckie asked, realizing just how important this man was.

"Yep," the farmer said.

"How did you two get separated?" Chuckie asked.

The farmer smiled wryly. "That's a whole 'nother story," he said, winking at Chuckie. Then he made his way out of the room.

Chuckie almost didn't notice. He pulled his wheelchair closer to Bingo's bed. He barely noticed as all of Bingo's friends spoke quiet words of encouragement.

Right then, there was only room in his heart for one thing — Bingo.

He reached the dog and carefully gave him a gentle hug. "Oh, Bingo!" he said. "You've just got to pull through! I need you boy!"

Bingo's eyes flew open. Chuckie gasped with joy.

"Oh, Bingo!" Chuckie said, his eyes filled with tears of joy.

"Woof!"